# SUZE'S DIARY

## A SIDEWINDERS COMPANION NOVELLA

### KAT MIZERA

# INTRODUCTION

Dear Readers:

This isn't a new book in the Sidewinders series. It's not a stand alone and you definitely don't want to read it if you haven't read at least the first two books in the Las Vegas Sidewinders series.

Since you only got to share Suze and Cody's story through the eyes of their friends, and one short Christmas novella, this is her diary. It starts right after the death of CJs biological father, Brian Barnett, who was also Suze's college sweetheart. You'll see what Suze went through losing Brian, finding out CJ wasn't Cody's son, falling in love with Cody, and finally getting to a point where she feels she doesn't need to write anymore.

So sit down with your favorite beverage and dig in—Suze's Diary fills in many of the gaps that you never got to see on the page and recaps a lot of events from this fifteen-book series that you may have forgotten.

Enjoy!

Love, Kat

1

———

## MAY 10, 2005

I'M PREGNANT.

Oh. My. God.

If I thought things couldn't get any worse, they just did.

I've taken ten tests.

All positive.

All a direct reflection of the spectacular disaster my life has become.

How could you leave me, Brian? Like, seriously, how could you do this to me? I've never cried so many tears or physically ached for someone the way I do for you. You swore to love and take care of me always. We had a plan, you bastard. We were supposed to get married this summer before you start your NHL career.

What is this death bullshit?

I'm so fucking pissed at you, Brian Barnett. I know it's not your fault, not really, but how could you leave me like this? And now I have to tell your best friend—whom I fucked in a car outside the bar we went to after your funeral—that I'm pregnant. So you've ruined my life and I'm about to ruin his.

I've never wanted to get drunk so badly in my life. Except I can't because, you know, there's a fucking baby.

A baby!

I can't even take care of myself. How the fuck am I going to take care of a baby? Cody will send money. I know that. But what about being a dad? Actually seeing his kid? How are we going to do that with him in Toronto and me home in South Carolina? At least if it was your baby, I could probably move in with your parents, but this is an epic clusterfuck. EPIC!

You and I always used condoms, without fail, so Cody and I must have been incredibly irresponsible. Well, we were drunk. Irresponsible doesn't touch on what we did. God, were we drunk. I just needed someone to touch me. To make me feel alive again for a few minutes, because I went completely numb during your funeral.

Completely, absolutely, 100% devoid of emotion.

One good orgasm shocked me back to reality. How's that for fucked up?

And ended up with a baby inside me to boot.

Are you mad yet? Are you anywhere near as mad as I am?

Of course not. You're dead.

Dammit, Brian, what am I going to do?

Cody's a good guy. I know he'll support his child, but who's going to support me?

# AUGUST, 2005

IT'S BEEN A FEW MONTHS SINCE I'VE WRITTEN IN THIS DIARY because my life has changed in ways that are hard to explain. When I told Cody I was pregnant, the last thing I expected was for him to ask me to marry him. Immediately. But he did and I did and here we are.

I guess I"m going to keep this diary as a way to document everything I'm feeling as I move forward without you, Brian. It's the only thing I can do. I wake up every day and put one foot in front of the other. There is no other direction to go.

Forward.

Without you.

Cody and I have been in Toronto for two months now and I think I'm finally learning my way around. Our apartment is great, big with lots of windows and underground parking. We've got a spare bedroom for the baby and Cody wants to start decorating soon. We definitely won't be able to stay here more than a year since we both want a house when the baby comes, but for now this is great and gives us time to figure out where we want to buy something. He's close to the arena and I'm in a busy, populated area with shopping, restaurants and night life. Not that I feel like going out at night.

I'm four months pregnant and although they say you get a burst of energy in the second trimester, I'm still waiting for that. I sleep a lot, but I guess that's okay because I don't really feel like doing anything. Cody and I met up with a couple of the other players and their wives for dinner last night and it was nice, but my eyes were starting to close by ten o'clock. Luckily, the other wives have been pregnant before so they were nice about it.

Cody and I have been married for a little over two months and it's going better than I thought it would. He's really sweet. He's doing great considering one minute he was single, the next he was married and having a kid. I haven't seen him get frustrated or impatient even once, and I know I've been a hormonal nightmare. But he just holds my hand or strokes my hair when I cry and tells me it's going to be okay. I just don't know how anything is ever going to be okay.

Brian's been gone four months. Four months since I've seen his smile or had his arms around me. Four months since those monsters killed him. Four months since I lost the love of my life. Cody doesn't know, but I have a tape from my answering machine with Brian's last couple of messages. When Cody's at the gym or out with friends I play it and listen to Brian's sweet voice; I don't know if I'll ever get past this. I miss him sooooo much. I talked to his mom, Andra, last night and we both cried.

Well, Cody will be back from the gym soon and we're going to Niagara Falls for the weekend, so I have to get going. Hoping it takes my mind off everything. He says we need to get away--I think he's ready to start having sex and I don't know what to do about that. Cody is gorgeous--tall and blond, with a face that should be on magazine covers. There's nothing wrong with him. It's just me. Missing Brian. Feeling fat and pregnant. Wanting to go back in time to when Brian was still alive and we had our whole future ahead of us. I don't know what to do with this wonderful man I call my husband but I don't feel anything for except friendship. My dead boyfriend's best friend. God, what have I gotten myself into?

3

# DECEMBER 31, 2005

I can't believe I'm a mom. Cody Brian Armstrong was born at 9:05 a.m. on December 29th. He was 8 pounds, 9 ounces and 21 inches long. He's got a whole bunch of super white fuzzy hair on his head and eyes that seem blue—just like mine and Cody's. We think we're going to call him CJ, even though technically he's not Cody Junior since Cody's middle name is John, but we think calling him Cody will get confusing and there's no way in hell we can call him Brian…

I'm a little bummed that the new house isn't ready yet, but we should close in a few weeks. My mom is coming in a few days to help out while Cody's on the road, and she'll stay until we move in. I'm really grateful because being a mom is pretty scary. Cody took a few days off when the baby was born, so we could have a little time together, just the three of us, to settle into being a family. I don't know how I feel about all of this, but CJ is the coolest thing that's ever happened to me. I didn't think I would ever love someone this much, but he's just this beautiful little bundle of love. When I look into his sweet face, all the pain of the last nine months fades just a little.

Even though things with Cody and I are still kind of weird, I have to say he was awesome throughout the pregnancy and birth.

He was at my side the whole time I was in labor, making jokes, holding my hand and making sure I had everything I needed. He didn't try to pretend like everything was going to be okay—he asked me what I needed from him and gave it to me. I don't know why he decided to step up and take care of us, but I'm so glad he did. Of course, he was Brian's best friend, but I just don't understand why he took it on himself. Yes, we had sex and got pregnant, but he didn't have to marry me and bring me to Toronto with him. He could've just sent money every month. That's not who he is, though. No, Cody's a better man than that. He wants to make sure we have everything we need, and he's going to make sure of that first-hand.

In the meantime, the new house is going to be amazing! It has four bedrooms, a pool and a big, airy kitchen. It's in a nice neighborhood with security gates and a playground. It's further from the arena than where we are now, but everyone we talked to says it's a great area with good schools and easy access to everything. We don't know how long we'll be here, but Cody said he wanted us to have a home, not just a place to live. See what I mean? He's so amazing and I don't get it—I don't understand why he's being so good to me. Even though it looks like CJ is his son, he didn't have to keep me too. I wish I understood all of this, but we're heading into a new year, a new home, a new beginning. I really, really hope it's better than last year.

## 4

# APRIL 2006

Sex. It's pretty much the elephant in the room. ALL. THE. TIME. It's not like Cody and I have never slept together, but we also didn't do anything except get drunk and fall into bed together. Well, it was more like his car outside the bar where we'd been drinking. So we're married and have a kid, but have only had sex once, in the back of his car. A car we don't even own anymore. We didn't even have sex on our honeymoon—I wasn't ready and he was gentleman enough not to push it. *Crap.*

Last night he tried to kiss me and I let him, but then I said no. I feel like a jerk. He deserves better. I just don't know what to do. It's been a year since we lost Brian and I know it's time to move on. Cody is wonderful—good-looking, kind, generous, and such a great dad. I watch the look on his face when he sees CJ after getting home from a trip and I fall a little bit in love with him every single time. I still miss Brian, but our new life in Toronto is pretty great. Our house is gorgeous and Cody told me to buy whatever I wanted. It was kind of scary at first—neither of us have ever had this kind of money—but we share the banking and the bills, so we know what we're doing and have a budget. A budget! I sound like a grown-up! Oh, well, I guess I'm married and a mom, so I should be a grown-up… it's just kind of weird.

CJ is growing so fast, almost four months old and smiling and gurgling and trying to make sounds. Cody is like a little kid with him, laying on the floor and staring at him for hours at a time. It's nice, because I get to have a little time to myself, but it's lonely too. I wish we were a real couple, enjoying our baby together. Instead, it's me and CJ or him and CJ. Sure, we have meals together and go out once in a while, but hockey keeps him busy and the baby keeps me busy. He's still not sleeping through the night, so I nap when he does and try to get as much done as I can when Cody's home.

I think the worst thing about Toronto is being lonely. I've met a few of the other wives but they're in real relationships, where they fell in love and got married. Everyone knows I was Brian Barnett's girl; everyone had been watching the hotshot goalie from Boston College. Then suddenly I was married to his best friend, and obviously people know there's a baby… if you put two and two together, I'm either a whore or a gold-digger. I'm not sure what's worse. Cody is super protective of me, and we tell the truth about having drunk sex after the funeral—after all, the only other options are whore and gold-digger. Ugh.

So sex or no sex? I mean, should I deprive both of us out of guilt? I don't know what to do. My mom says go for it; my friends from college say I'm being silly. I wish I knew what Brian would want me to do. I know he would want me to be happy, but happy was with *him*. Without him, I don't know how to be happy. Do I?

5

———

## JULY 2006

Summer vacation sure doesn't mean the same thing when you're a married parent that it did when you were a single college student. With hockey season over and Cody home all the time, it's different around the house. We go to bed together, we wake up together, we do things with CJ together… it's like being a real couple. Except we're not. And yeah, we started having sex. He's pretty amazing, even though I'm having a little trouble with it. Not the sex itself—that's awesome—but after. I always think about Brian and wonder what he would say if he was here. Then I remember that if he was here, I wouldn't be with Cody. How fucked up is that???

I don't know what to think sometimes. Life is good. Life is almost great. And Brian is in that awful cemetery in Boston, becoming one with nature. He was 22. He was signed to the Bruins and had a bright future ahead of him. He was just about to graduate with a degree in engineering. Brian was the whole package—smart, good-looking, athletic, talented, strong, and soooo romantic. He was everything to me and moving on like he never existed feels wrong on so many levels. I want so much to be able to talk to Cody about how I feel, but I can see the hurt in his eyes whenever Brian's name comes up. I guess he's grieving in his own way and I'm still too raw to help with that.

We got some weird news today: Our friends from college, Sergei and Maria, are moving to Russia. They eloped yesterday and got on a plane to Moscow. Sergei is going to play in the KHL and I guess Maria is going to be a Russian housewife. I don't think she's going to be very happy, but I never thought they were a good couple anyway. Sergei was never the kind of guy that slept around much, but he always treated Maria like an afterthought. I was shocked when they got serious, and hearing they got married makes me wonder if something's going on with him.

Dom is coming to visit next week and I'm really looking forward to seeing him. He didn't have a great year in the NHL this season, so I hope the boys can do some bonding and Cody can help him get his head on straight. I think we're all still grieving while we pretend to move on and I don't believe any of us are truly happy. I keep thinking I should go talk to someone, a therapist or something, but I'm afraid it would hurt Cody's feelings. Maybe when hockey season starts I can do it without him knowing… is that wrong? I'm not trying to go behind his back but I just don't know what to do with all these feelings. I'm so confused. I want to be happy—I want to fall in love with him—but something is holding me back. Brian is right there between us—in bed, in my head and I think in Cody's head too. He's just too much of a guy to admit it.

Thank goodness for CJ. If there's anything that's going right in my life it's this seven-month-old blue-eyed angel who steals my heart every time he says, "Mama" or giggles, or falls asleep on my chest. I love being a mom. I wasn't sure what it was going to be like, especially considering how I got pregnant, but I shouldn't have worried. He's just a doll and I love him to death. Cody does too, which is really great. If only we were a real family… I hope CJ never finds out how messed up his parents are or we can find a way to make things right before he's old enough to notice.

After Dom leaves we're going on vacation. Cody's parents are coming to stay with CJ and we're going to New York City for four days. Cody thinks taking me shopping will make me happy… he doesn't understand that I just need to feel secure again, like I know what's going to happen in my life instead of waking up every day wondering who I am and whether or not I belong here. This just doesn't feel like my life; I feel like an imposter, some girl who got knocked up and took over Cody Armstrong's life. I mean, really—why would he be sacrificing so much for someone he had a one-night-stand with? He was close to Brian, and I was Brian's girl, but it seems like he's doing more than he should. I'm afraid one day he's going to wake up and realize how much he gave up for me, and ask for a divorce. I don't know how I would stand it.

Well, I'm going to go soak in the tub and try to clear my head. Some days the pain is overwhelming and this is the only place I can talk about it.

# CHRISTMAS 2006

TECHNICALLY, THIS IS OUR SECOND CHRISTMAS AS A MARRIED couple but last year I was nine months pregnant and we were going through so much: adjusting to Toronto, life as an NHL wife, pregnancy, getting ready for a baby, house hunting, etc. This year is totally different. My mom is here, as well as Cody's parents, and CJ is going to be one spoiled little boy! Between Christmas and his upcoming first birthday—you've never seen so much crap everywhere! It's really fun, though.

Having the family around is nice because Cody and I don't have to be "alone" all the time and we do well when we're with family and friends. Cody bought me a ring—a real freakin' engagement ring since the one he originally got me was cubic zirconia. This baby is three karats in a platinum setting and it's like nothing I ever dreamed about. Although no one knew our ring was C.Z. it was still just one karat and he wanted me to be like the other wives—even though he knows I don't care that much, there have apparently been some comments made about my "cute little ring" that got back to him through guys on the team.

He also got me, my mom and his mom a day at the spa next week! It's going to be great... I've never been to one, and that's something else the wives all talk about, so he's trying to help me fit in without saying so. I don't know if he knows that I know what he's up to… but it's sweet anyway. He's doing so much to help me get through the changes in our lives, I wish I could do something for him. I bought him a very expensive leather jacket similar to something he had in college that's falling apart and I think he really likes it. CJ bought him a set of CJ-sized hockey sticks with a foam puck that I "autographed" from CJ and he got a little teary-eyed. He's really the best dad ever.

Things have improved a little in the bedroom emotionally, but I'm still holding back. I don't know how to make things better. The physical part is fine—although I think he's holding back because I used to listen to them talk when Brian was still alive and, even though I know he's done it with other women, he's never thrown me against the wall and fucked me standing up. We're pretty much all about missionary, on the bed, late at night. There's no passion and I don't know which one of us is responsible… is it me? Because I'm the woman and he's being a gentleman? Is it him because he thinks he needs to tread carefully? What is it, exactly, making him treat me with kid gloves? I know I should say something, but how do you say it? Uh, honey, you're kind of boring in bed and I'd love you to be a little more passionate? He's not selfish at all—he always makes sure I get off first—but it's very vanilla. Brian and I were all over the place —the wall, the shower, the floor, and holy shit, when Brian went down on me I couldn't even think straight. Cody's never done that—and I've never gone down on him. It's like high school again, tentative and careful. It feels good, and he always satisfies me, but something is missing. Sigh…

Anyway, I've got to get some sleep. We have stuff going on every day this week until everyone leaves on the first of January! I'm hoping the New Year will bring some new excitement to the bedroom.

# APRIL 1, 2007

I DREAMED ABOUT BRIAN LAST NIGHT. WE WERE IN HIS apartment on campus, cuddled up in bed like we used to be almost every morning our senior year. He woke up first and started to kiss me. He was whispering how much he loved me and how he couldn't wait for me to give birth to his son... when I woke up it was like it had been real. Except Brian and I never had a conversation about me being pregnant because he'd never gotten me pregnant. At least I didn't think he had. Until yesterday, when I looked deep into CJ's eyes and felt like I was looking at Brian's beautiful grey eyes. Eyes that had been blue until recently. I don't know what to do because Cody and I both have really blue eyes. I know it's possible for two blue-eyed parents to have a child with a different color but it's not very likely. What's much more likely is that CJ isn't Cody's son and that I was already pregnant when Cody and I had sex the night of the funeral.

I don't know how to tell Cody, but he's not stupid and he's going to notice if he hasn't already. If CJ isn't Cody's, what the hell am I going to do? I have no idea if he's going to want to stay married or if he's going to throw me out. I guess I don't really believe that—he wouldn't do that to me and he loves that little boy. But this could be a game changer and it scares the hell out of me. I don't know what I'll do if I have to move home to South Carolina. I got my degree but there aren't any jobs in my home town and I can't afford to live on my own.

I 'm already a mess and Cody probably thinks it's because today is Brian's birthday. It would have been his 24th and it's the second anniversary of his death. Hard to believe he's been gone two years already… two long years without talking to him or watching him play hockey or feeling him touch me. I've started getting used to Cody touching me, but he's still so damn tentative. It's gotten a little better, but I have a feeling telling him we need to get a paternity test isn't going to help things.

W hy does everything have to be so hard? Sometimes I get so fucking pissed off that Brian left me. I know he didn't want to, but dammit, why did he have to die? Why didn't Cody, Dom and Sergei walk back to the apartment with him? Why did they wait half an hour to go looking for him? Why were those gang bangers in that particular alley? I'll never have any answers and that's what pisses me off the most. My mom says I should get therapy—and she's probably right—but I don't want to. All that's going to do is dredge up the pain all over again and I'm finally getting to a point where I can go a few days without missing him. Is therapy really going to change anything? I can't believe it will make me stop missing him or help my relationship with Cody.

I know I should try… but I'm just not ready to open myself up like that. Not yet. Part of me wonders if talking to a professional will help me handle telling Cody that he's not CJ's father but another part of me feels like I should just get it out in the open. If he's going to throw us out, I need to know sooner rather than later.

Holy shit—he might actually throw us out. I can't even fathom living without him now that we've been together almost two years. Fuck fuck fuck. I have to talk to him. Today. What a day to bring this up. Shit. Brian, how the hell did we get pregnant?! We slept together for more than three years and had our only accident on the day you died? How the hell does that happen! I wish you were here to tell me how we managed to do that? I'm really mad at you right now, Brian. Really, really mad.

8

# JUNE 2007

I CRIED FOR A LONG TIME TODAY. TODAY IT WAS OFFICIAL. Today we found out for sure. CJ is not Cody's son; CJ is *Brian's* son. When the registered letter came in the mail, I froze. I knew what it was and I couldn't move. Cody signed for it and pulled me into the family room. We sat on the couch and he looked at me and said, "This is just a piece of paper, Suze. It doesn't change anything."

Of course it changes things! I haven't cried this hard since the moment they took Brian off the ventilator at the hospital. I couldn't stop. It got so bad that Cody called our babysitter to watch CJ and took me out of the house. We sat on a bench at the park and I cried for at least two hours. Cody just stroked my hair and held me as tight as he could. He had tears in his eyes when he first read the results too, but then he manned up so he could take care of me. I couldn't truly appreciate it at the moment, but now that I'm thinking about it, I see what he did—he hid the pain of finding out CJ wasn't his son so he could help me get through it.

When I finally got up the nerve to ask him if he was going to leave us, he looked at me like I was an idiot. He told me he was never leaving us, that CJ and I were his family and the fact that it was Brian who actually got me pregnant didn't matter to him—he loved Brian and he loved us and I should stop thinking that way. I was a wreck all day, but I'm calmer now. We went out to dinner and walked around by the lake. Then we came home and made love, like a real couple. Tonight wasn't about sex, though, it was about emotion and bonding and I think he was trying to show me that he wanted to make this work between us. I'm still pretty shaken up, but it was good to hear him say that he was never leaving us.

Of course, now I have to tell Brad and Andra. It's been two years since Brian died and they're going to have to re-open all those wounds when they find out he had a son. I hate doing that to them because they went through a rough time too. I heard through the grapevine that they separated, that Andra was dating some 18-year-old player from Kingston, Ontario and Brad was going from strip club to strip club. Dom said they're in counseling now, but he didn't know any details.

Dom's a mess, too. Quiet and almost surly. Cody talks to him every few months but he seems to be pulling away from us, from everyone, really. I wish he would tell us what's wrong. I'm worried about him but he always laughs and says he's fine. We might meet up in the Bahamas in August, and if we do, I'll try to get inside his head, the big oaf. Of course, if I didn't have Dom and Sergei to worry about, I'd spend all my time feeling sorry for myself.

I'm not sure what all of this means, you know? I'm living someone else's life—someone that loved Cody, not Brian. I still feel like an imposter and I don't know why. I'm trying really hard to get past all of this, but some days it feels futile. I'm so confused and heartbroken, it feels like Brian just died all over again. And now I can't help but wonder what Brian would think of our son. Would he love him like I do? Would he be a good dad? Deep down, I know the answers, but there's a part of me searching for a tangible response.

It's weird when I think about him sometimes. We talked about our future, but we never talked specifically about kids. Yes, we wanted them someday, but Brian never talked about wanting a son or daughter and I couldn't even imagine becoming a mom while I was still in college. Cody, on the other hand, talked about how much he wanted a little boy all the time. Not when we were in college, but from the moment he found out I was pregnant. It was like he stepped into the role without having to think twice and I find it an ironic twist of fate that he wound up raising his best friend's son. Such a good guy and I think he got a raw deal getting stuck with me.

Sometimes I wonder who Cody loved all through college. I know there was someone—every so often he would look at Brian and I and get this really sweet, faraway look in his eyes that told me he had feelings for someone. There wasn't anyone obvious, but there had to be someone. I wonder who she is and if she loved him too. Was she heartbroken when she found out he married me? Mad that he got me pregnant? I asked him once and he laughed, said there were a lot of girls, but no one in particular —when did he have time?

I hope this whole situation didn't break his heart the way it broke mine because my life is sad enough and I don't want that for him. One of us should be happy again and it probably isn't going to be me.

9
_______

SEPTEMBER 2007

CODY AND I HAD OUR FIRST REAL FIGHT TODAY. IT WAS PRETTY epic, too. We yelled until we woke CJ from his nap and then we were both so frustrated Cody left and went for a drive. It was definitely my fault. He was going golfing with some teammates and I was up all night with CJ, who was throwing up, so I asked him if he could please just *pretend* to be a dad and give me a hand since I didn't sleep last night. Of course he threw it back in my face that he's *not* a dad and then I don't even know what happened after that. It was awful.

He apologized when he came home, and didn't go golfing, but there's definitely a distance between us now. He went up to bed hours ago but I'm still downstairs, staring at the TV. I don't know where to go from here. We've never had a real fight before. He's always so easy-going and happy, able to talk me down when I'm having a bad day or cheer me up when I'm grumpy. Not lately, though. Something definitely broke when we found out CJ wasn't his, and even though he doesn't take it out on him, the distance between us is becoming something I can almost see.

My mom thinks we need an adult get-away, but I don't have

it in me right now. I'm tired. CJ is into everything and although Cody really is a good dad, he's always working out or hanging out with his teammates. He's home for breakfast and dinner every night when he's not on the road, and once in a while I get to go out with one of the girls, but mostly he's gone all day and I'm alone. I haven't really bonded with any of the other wives and I don't know why. I had friends in high school and college, but when I met Brian he was all I needed. I had him, but I also had his friends. Dom, Cody and Sergei were my friends too, so I didn't have a lot of time for girlfriends. Now it seems like maybe I don't know how to have female friends.

I have a few, but not anyone I'm close to. Certainly no one I can talk to about Cody. The only person I can talk to is my mom and she's annoying because she adores Cody and says most of our problems are my fault, that I'm hanging on to Brian and not giving Cody a chance. Maybe she's right. I don't want to forget Brian. I don't want to love his best friend. I don't want this life —I want the one we were going to have together.

It's not Cody's fault. This is all me. He tries really hard to make me happy, but with me grieving and so fucking lonely, and him always at practice or on the road, I don't know how to bridge this distance between us. The sex is almost forced, like we go through the motions, but without the romance it's one step better than masturbation. We rub each other until we get off. Done. He's always gentle and kind, of course, but that's not the same. It doesn't have the excitement or passion of a one-night stand either, so we're in this weird in-between area that kind of sucks.

I keep thinking that I should give him his freedom, let him find someone who'll love him the way he should be loved. But then what will I do? How would I take care of CJ? Even if Cody sent child support, I'd still have to work and we'd have to live in South Carolina, which is far from Toronto. I don't want that for CJ, and honestly, I can't imagine being without Cody. I do have feelings for him—I'm just not in love with him. The big question is whether or not I ever could be...and could he ever love me? Until we sort that out, I don't think we can do anything.

10

# JANUARY 1, 2008

Happy New Year to me. Cody's on the road and our parents have all headed home. So I'm sitting in my beautiful house, with my beautiful little boy, all alone, feeling really ugly on the inside. The holidays sucked. Cody and I have done nothing but fight for months. We put on a good act while the family was around, and of course CJ's birthday was lovely, but the rest of the time we're grumpy and short with each other. Something is bound to give soon, and maybe it's time we call it quits. I don't think I can live like this and I'm afraid it's going to affect Cody's playing. He hasn't been as much of a force on the ice lately, and I think it's because of everything going on at home.

On the bright side, we went to a holiday party last month at the home of one of the other guys on the team, Shawn Hampton, and his wife and I hit it off. Her name is Paula and she's sweet. They've only been married six months and she just found out she's pregnant, so she's kind of freaked out and I was able to make her feel better. I can't talk about anything going on in my life, so it feels a little one-sided, but that's not her fault. It'll be nice to have someone to talk to, even if I skirt around the issues with Cody. Of course, if Cody and I get a divorce, I'll have to leave Toronto so it won't matter.

I don't know what to do. We live in this big, gorgeous house and have this incredible life with fancy vacations and the best of everything…but when it's just the two of us, it feels like we're coming undone. Everything is strained, and the easy camaraderie we've had since college is gone. We fight or bicker constantly, and I turn away from him when we're in bed because I just can't do it anymore. It feels wrong and it's like I've been faking it. I know he's getting sick of me turning him down, too. The weird thing is, I get kind of sick to my stomach just thinking about leaving him.

If I wanted to, I could move home to South Carolina and find a job. It wouldn't be a great job, but I would find something. CJ will start pre-school this coming Fall so child care won't be too bad and I wouldn't have to pay rent to live with Mama. I know Cody would send child support, so we'd be okay, but when I try to actually make it a realistic plan, I can't imagine leaving Cody. I'm not sure why I feel this way since all we do is fight. The truth is that he's my best friend. We're not getting along right now but I know that's mostly my fault and he's doing the best he can. There is no universe I can imagine where Cody and I aren't friends, and that's what makes this so hard.

He'll be home in a few days and I'm going to try to talk to him even though it's scary. I really don't want a divorce, but I want to be prepared just in case. I've done some research to find an online program where I can get my MBA. I know Cody won't hesitate to pay for it, so I think I'll use it as a bargaining chip— tell him it will take me two years to get my Master's and by then CJ will be starting Kindergarten. When I've got the degree, and the opportunity for a better job, we can discuss separating or getting a divorce. Ugh. Divorce! That's a horrible word. But what choice do I have? I can't be what he seems to want—which is a real wife—and he's never going to be Brian.

*Brian.* Shit. He's been gone almost three years and I still talk to him, miss him, think about him. I guess I'm not doing a good job of moving on, but that's a joke. When someone old dies, you feel bad and you miss them, but it's not a surprise. This, well, this was a whole other thing and I'm still really angry. I read about the stages of grief and I don't find myself going through them.

There was never any denial…we saw him stop breathing when they turned off life support. I was holding his hand and I felt the life drain out of him, so there was no time for denial. And anger—damn, it's been almost three years and I'm still angry as hell. Bargaining? What the hell is that? Uh, if Brian comes back from the dead I'll stop eating ice cream? Work out more? Give up all my money? I mean, what kind of bullshit is that?! And then there's depression. Sure, I have a little but I'm still too pissed off to give in to depression. So I'm a long fucking way from ACCEPTANCE.

Right this second, I'm back to ANGRY. Angry as hell. At him for being so scatter-brained he forgot the ring. At those thugs for hurting him for no reason. At Dom, Cody and Sergei for letting him go by himself. At myself for planning the party that brought him out for the night. Now what? Is anyone listening? What the fuck do I do now?

11

## APRIL 2, 2008

I did a dumb thing yesterday. I went to Brian's grave. Cody was on the road with the team and a couple of the wives and I decided to go with them and make a shopping trip out of it. We had a great time in New York City while they played the Rangers and the Devils, but then we came down to Boston. What a mistake that was. I knew the minute we got in the rental car I was going to be a wreck. Since I'd lived in the area for four years, I was in charge of driving and I found myself headed right for our old stomping grounds.

The BU campus looks the same and I was careful not to show any emotion while we drove past it, but when I asked if we could take a detour the girls were all great about it. I should have known better, but I had to see him. *Him.* Like he's really there, buried underground, just waiting for me to save him. I know it's silly but I couldn't seem to help myself. I told them to wait in the car, that I'd be right back. Yeah, that didn't happen.

I looked down at the words written on that headstone and lost my shit. I don't know what happened, but I cried so hard Paula had to come get me. I didn't realize she knew the story of me, Brian and Cody, so not only did I make a fool of myself, but I potentially could have hurt Cody's career too if she hadn't been so kind. Paula was great, though, helping me get myself under control before we went back to the car. Paula took over driving and I just huddled in the front seat trying not to go nuts. It was the first time I understood the words "he's never coming back." It's been three freakin' years and I'm just now discovering he's not coming back? That's pathetic.

The other wives were confused, but they did the best they could to comfort me. I had no choice but to tell them my college boyfriend had been killed just before graduation and they were wonderful. Unfortunately, Paula told Shawn and Shawn told Cody, and he was really upset with me when we met up at the hotel that night. He said I embarrassed him, and he was right, but I started crying again and instead of walking away, he just held me. All night. Until I finally had to tell him he needed to rest.

It's funny, he didn't say a word the entire night. Then this morning when I woke up he was sitting in a chair by the window, just staring at nothing. I asked him what was wrong and he looked at me with something in his eyes I'd never seen before: Defeat. I don't know if he felt like he'd failed me, failed our marriage or somehow failed himself, but he looked so sad it broke my heart. I hope I never see anyone look that sad ever again.

We made some decisions, though. He told me to go ahead and start taking classes so I could get my master's degree. He said he would do whatever I wanted, but he didn't think letting anyone know CJ wasn't his was a good idea. So we agreed that we would keep things relatively the same for two more years while I got another degree and we took care of CJ. The only difference was that we weren't going to share a bed anymore. We would keep our things in the master bedroom, just the way they were, but when I said I would sleep in the guest room he got really mad. He said he was the one on the road all the time and that I should take the main bedroom. When he was home, he'd sleep in the guest room or on the couch, and no one needed to know our business.

The only thing he asked of me was for me to start seeing a therapist. He said he'd do anything I wanted if I promised to do that, so I said I would. I also told him he didn't have to be faithful to me since we weren't sharing a bed anymore. I told him to be discreet and not embarrass me, but I understand that he has needs that I can't fulfill.

He looked like I'd slapped him when I said that, but then he just nodded. As if his only concern in the world is my well-being. What in holy hell is wrong with me? Why do I keep pushing away this wonderful man who tries so hard to make me happy? This is definitely not what I had in mind when we got married, but there doesn't seem to be a choice. I'm going to have to focus on school and making a plan for two years from now.

12

AUGUST 2008

There's nothing that can make your troubles seem far away like a trip to Hawaii. We're here on Oahu, staying at this amazing resort in Waikiki, and it's like I don't have a care in the world. Seriously, we got here two days ago and checked in. We had something to eat and then, after that ridiculously long flight, we were wiped and all went to bed.

We were up early yesterday and we had room service deliver breakfast. Then Cody had CJ set up for some toddler surfing/swimming thing here at the resort while we got a couple's massage followed by a gourmet lunch with champagne and truffles, and a swim in this private cove with all kinds of sea life. It was the most relaxing, romantic and thoughtful afternoon ever. I almost started to cry. Cody said he felt bad about how distant we'd been lately, and even though we weren't going to be a real couple, he wanted us to be best friends again. I bawled when he said that, and then he hugged me really tight. Right before he made love to me on the private balcony of our room. I had an epic orgasm, which was unfortunately followed by another fit of hysterical crying on my part.

Seriously, I have to wonder if there's something wrong with me. And as usual, Cody just held on to me, let me cry and reminded me that he'd made a promise to always take care of me and he intended to keep it. Even if I didn't want to sleep with him anymore, he didn't want me to leave. Not now, not in two years, not when CJ left for college. He promised he wouldn't touch me again, but he just wanted me to know he would always be here for me.

And then, because I wasn't messed up enough, he got up and got dressed and went on with his day like nothing had happened. We picked up CJ from the club and went to dinner. This morning, he ordered another amazing room service breakfast and announced that Dom was arriving this afternoon to spend a few days with us. He asked if it was okay if they went golfing tomorrow morning, but said he had another activity set up for CJ so the three of us could go on a private snorkeling excursion when they were done!

So I'm laying here at the pool watching CJ frolic in the water with some other kids (all being watched by lifeguards so us lazy moms can just work on our tans). Cody and Dom are golfing, CJ is having a blast, and I'm...well, I'm relaxed. Nothing has changed. Except I managed to have one incredible orgasm and got a few startling revelations from my husband. Something about the whole trip has been cathartic, though. Maybe it's because we're in Hawaii. It just feels like the weight of the world has been lifted and I don't know why. I definitely felt all kinds of confused making love with Cody again after so many months, but he promised he wouldn't do that again and I honestly don't know how I feel about that.

But because we're in Hawaii, I'm not going to think about it. Nope. I'm going to lay here in the sun, watch my kid play and then go snorkeling this afternoon with my husband and our friend. Tomorrow, well, I'll worry about all that other stuff then.

# OCTOBER 2008

I STARTED TAKING ONLINE CLASSES FOR MY MASTER'S DEGREE. I'm just taking one right now, trying to make sure I don't overwhelm myself and get back into the swing of studying and writing papers. I have to say, being back in school, but online, is a totally different vibe. I miss late-night study sessions and coffee dates to talk philosophy and hanging out after class…it's different than actually being in a classroom and on campus. I'm enjoying it, though. Cody's busy with hockey and CJ is in school three days a week, so it's nice to have me time that has nothing to do with the house or the boys. This is all about doing something entirely for myself and it's fun. Never thought I'd miss thinking and studying!

I don't know exactly what an MBA is going to do for me, but I figure it should open a few doors if I was ever forced to get a job, right? Cody says I don't have to worry about that, he's never going to leave me on my own, but I still want to be able to take care of myself if I have to. I mean, we're a marriage in name only now, so I should be prepared for anything. Mama thinks I should secretly put money away somewhere, a little at a time, just in case, but that feels smarmy. It's his money and even though I don't have a problem buying a new pair of shoes or something for the house, hiding money just feels wrong.

It's enough that he's paying for my education and gives me and my son a good life. Huh. Look at that—I called him *my* son instead of *our* son. Cody would be pissed if he heard me say that, because no matter what, he adores that little boy. The way they giggle and carry on when they're together is so sweet, I can't help but watch.

It's weird not having Cody beside me at night anymore. He sleeps in the guest room or on the couch, although he's always careful to get up before CJ. The other night we were up late because of a leak in the kitchen so he collapsed on the bed next to me, afraid that CJ would wake up first and find us in separate rooms. I have to admit I'd missed it and part of me wishes he was there every night again, like before. I just don't know how to tell him I was wrong, that I miss the intimacy. Intimacy means sex, though, and even though it's good when we do it, the aftermath is more than I can handle. Even after more than three years, I still feel guilty, like I'm cheating on Brian. I really hope I get past that someday…never having sex again would suck.

All in all, though, life is pretty good and I don't want to rock the boat. We have money, friends, our health and each other. I guess I should be grateful, because so many people don't have what we have. That's my new mantra: Be Grateful. I don't always believe it, but I repeat it over and over, especially moments like right now, when I can hear CJ's sweet laughter as Cody tickles him before bed. I should go in there and tell him to stop getting him riled up when he's supposed to be settling down, but I can't. I cherish these moments too much. I'm grateful that I get these moments. It could be so much worse. And maybe if I say it enough, I'll start to believe it.

$$14$$

# VALENTINE'S DAY, 2009

Valentine's Day has been kind of strange since I've been married. Technically, Cody and I aren't in love, so it feels weird to celebrate a holiday based on romance. He always sends me the biggest bouquets of flowers and buys me beautiful gifts—especially if he's on the road. The one year he was home we went out for a wonderful dinner. It's nice knowing that he's going to bend over backwards to make me happy, even for something as silly as Valentine's Day.

He's home today and actually has the day off. I woke up to breakfast in bed and lots of love and cuddles from CJ, who made me the cutest card at pre-school. After breakfast, Cody took CJ to school and told me to get ready. When he got back he took me shopping. I told him I didn't need anything but he wouldn't take no for an answer and, holy shit, did he spoil me! Diamond earrings, a Prada purse, a new dress for a team party we're going to in a few weeks, and three pairs of shoes. It had been embarrassing at first, but when I saw the genuine happiness in his eyes, I decided to let it go. I never know what he's thinking and sometimes it's just easier not to try to read his mind.

It was a nice afternoon. We had lunch and then headed out to pick up CJ. CJ decided he wanted pizza for dinner, so we ordered in and sat on the floor of the family room eating pizza and watching cartoons with him until bedtime. When he was finally settled, Cody and I watched a grown-up movie and went to bed. Separately, of course. He kissed my forehead and said he hoped I'd had a good day. Then he went in the other direction and left me alone in this big, empty bed with the TV and my diary.

I feel like an idiot. After nearly four years of marriage and eight years of friendship, it shouldn't be this hard. I should be able to have sex with my husband without thinking of someone else. I should be able to move on from my college sweetheart— he's been gone almost four freakin' years! I want another baby and I'm 99% sure Cody would be on board for that. I want to be in a real relationship, not this farce we call a marriage of convenience. Yet here I am. Alone in my bed, lonelier than I've ever been in my life, and really confused about everything.

I have to do something. Something has to give. Soon. I'm grateful I have someone taking care of me and that my son has a father, but how do we go on like this? How do we continue to dance around each other, as though this is normal? No matter what Cody says, I'm scared. Scared that he's going to change his mind. Scared that he's actually going to meet someone and fall in love and tell me we're done. Scared that I'm starting to have feelings for him even though I know he doesn't love me back. Scared that I'm going to get hurt. I'm going to see a therapist next week; maybe it will help. *Maybe.*

15

---

## MAY 2009

I KNEW HE WAS GOING TO BREAK MY HEART THE MINUTE I started to trust him. I knew it. And today's heartbreak was epic. Cody got back from a road trip late last night. There was a storm that delayed the flight so he didn't get home until 3:00 a.m. I let him sleep this morning since they have the day off and I snuck into his room to get his laundry so I could take it to the dry cleaners. His phone was on the dresser and it was buzzing like crazy. I grabbed it so it wouldn't wake him up and that's when the picture flashed on the screen. Some bimbo sent him a picture of her boobs—followed by a long, gushy post about how he'd rocked her world last weekend.

Ironically, he doesn't have any kind of lock code on his phone because he's always said he has no secrets—I guess that changed but since I've never had any reason to look at his phone before, he probably didn't even think about it. So I stood there for a few minutes, staring at the screen and reading these messages from Ally. Whoever the fuck that is. Someone he met on the last road trip, obviously. It's the playoffs and they won both games, so I guess he was ready to celebrate.

When I couldn't take it anymore, I put the phone down and slipped out of his room. Since CJ was at school, I called one of my friends and asked if she wanted to meet me for lunch. Then we went shopping. Damn, I'm a royal bitch when I'm upset. Ten thousand dollars later, I had a slight buzz from all the wine at lunch, I had more bags than I could carry and my friend Cleo was staring at me as if I'd lost my ever-loving mind. Which I have, of course.

Cody had picked up CJ up from school and they were putting a puzzle together on the floor when I got home. Cody got up to help me with the bags and I could see the confusion on his face as he stared at everything. I didn't say a word either. I kissed CJ and announced I was going to take a nap. I locked myself in my room and cried until I couldn't anymore. When I calmed down, I stood under a hot shower for a long time, until the water ran cold, and I'd steeled my resolve. I have a kid to take care of, and I'm getting my MBA. I don't have time to worry about Cody and his bimbos. And maybe Mama is right: I should be putting away some money. Just in case. I have to think of CJ. Even though Cody would send child support, CJ definitely wouldn't have all the things he has now if I have to start over somewhere. I definitely couldn't stay in Toronto, so I'd most likely wind up back in South Carolina, where good jobs are scarce.

I'm calling my therapist tomorrow so she can talk me off this ledge. Technically, I gave Cody the green light to sleep with other women, but it wasn't supposed to hurt this much. I wasn't supposed to see pictures on his phone. And I definitely wasn't supposed to start falling for him after I told him we couldn't be a couple. It's official: I'm an idiot.

16

# AUGUST, 2009

This is definitely a first. It's summer and I'm on vacation —nothing new about that—but I'm alone. Well, technically that's not true; I'm with my mom, my mom's friend Lula and my cousin Tippy. We're at this really great resort in Jamaica. No Cody, no CJ, just us girls. Cody took CJ to Minnesota to see his parents for a week and I'm here with the girls. Trying desperately not to slit my wrists. Not literally, of course, but this sure isn't the vacation we usually take every year. Hell, this whole summer has been miserable.

Cody went to Sweden for two weeks for some kind of intense summer skating workshop with some of his teammates, and then we spent July 4th weekend with a group of his teammates in the Hamptons. A couple of weeks ago he suggested I go somewhere with some of my girlfriends, but the truth is I don't really have anyone here I'm close enough to for that. So he offered to pay for my mom, aunt and cousin to go with me to a beach resort since he knows how much I love the beach. It was on the tip of my tongue to ask him why he didn't want to go, but then he launched into a speech about how he doesn't see his parents enough and how CJ barely knows them. Next thing I know, I'm in Jamaica, he's in Minnesota and this is probably the worst vacation of my life.

It's beautiful, of course, and we've had some fun—Mama can make a twenty-dollar hooker blush with her jokes—but it's not like being away with Cody. I miss his sweet smile, the way he used to look at me, the way he'd pull my chair out for me… ah, but I screwed that up pretty good, didn't I? I pushed him right into the arms of an endless supply of bimbos and now he doesn't spend much time with me at all. After I found those pictures on his phone he apologized, and said he'd be more discreet, but that was it. He didn't say he'd stop or ask me if I wanted to try again—he just apologized for getting caught. How fucked up is that? The worst part is that I told him to do it. I told him I wouldn't have sex with him anymore. I told him he was free to do whatever he wanted as long as he took care of CJ and me. I gave him permission to break my heart. Dear God, I'm a special kind of stupid.

It'll be easier when hockey season starts again. Even though he'll be on the road with lots of opportunity to cheat, at least he won't be underfoot breaking my heart every time he looks at me. And I'll be back in school, losing myself in a degree I neither want nor need. How the hell did I get to this place?

Mama read me the riot act and she's right, of course, but I'll be damned if I admit it to her or anyone else. Instead, I'm sitting here on the beach watching Mama and Lula hit on cabana boys half their age and Tippy sleeping with everything that moves. They say I should too—if Cody's doing it there's no reason I shouldn't—but that's not who I am. I gave him permission but technically he didn't do the same for me and it feels like cheating. I'm truly not the type to party. I had one boyfriend in high school and Brian and I met freshman year of college. Those are the only two guys I was ever with before Cody, and honestly, sleeping around sounds fun in theory, but I don't think it's for me. I obviously get way too attached, way too easily, and my fragile heart couldn't take another beating. I definitely have to talk to Cody. If only I knew what to say.

## OCTOBER, 2009

I sat Cody down last night and told him we needed to talk. Hockey season starts this week and there have to be some ground rules. Not only that, we couldn't continue to live the way we've been since the night I saw those pictures on his phone. It's been awkward and uncomfortable and hard on everyone. We live together, have a family together, and a little boy who needs us to be happy and healthy. Or at least as close to that as possible. He apologized again, said he would never do anything to embarrass me and that he was only doing what he thought I wanted by keeping his distance. He actually said he "wanted us to be friends again." I don't even know what the hell that means. Friends?! We're married, parents and, despite the current cluster-fuck, have been sleeping together on and off for four years.

Every time I think about telling him that I want us to be a couple, I remember that I wasn't his *choice*, that we're only married because he and Brian were so close. He didn't pick me, he just got stuck with his dead buddy's pregnant girlfriend. And even then, he wouldn't have married me if we hadn't gotten drunk and had sex the night of the funeral, resulting in what was possibly his kid. So I bite my tongue and do the best I can. I think he could see how much the distance between us has bothered me, though, so tonight we actually had our first date night in months.

We got a sitter for CJ and went to a little bistro we love. We talked for hours, finally getting to a place where we could laugh and feel like friends again. He even said he wants me to be happy, that he's sorry our being married is such a burden to me. To me?! I'm not the one sleeping around, buddy... but that might be what he meant. I don't know, because I'm too damn scared to ask him anything honest!

I don't know what to do next but maybe I need to just go with the flow for once. I spend way too much time worrying about what he's doing, thinking, feeling... it might be time for me to just live my own life. It's going to be a delicate balance, because we're married but not a couple in the traditional sense of the word. So that means being careful what I say and do publicly. He's sworn he'll be careful—no more texts or giving out his phone number—which is important to me. The weird thing is, I was anxious for us to stop sleeping together but now I miss it. Until today, when I started writing this journal entry, I hadn't thought about Brian in weeks. That's the first time since he died that I haven't thought about him almost every day. Does this mean I'm moving on? Am I finally starting to get past the pure anguish of knowing I'll never see him again? It's the weirdest feeling ever. It really is. I'll never forget him, but somehow over the summer it occurred to me that missing him does nothing but hurt me. I see him every time I look into CJ's steel-gray eyes, but I don't yearn for him anymore. No, now I yearn for Cody. My husband. The guy I told to start sleeping with other women. Yeah, I'm a mess.

18

# JANUARY, 2010

It's a brand-new year and this one is going to be better! I've decided. That was my New Year's resolution as well: No more pouting, no more dwelling on the past, no more negativity. Life has been better. Not great, but better. I don't know what, if anything, Cody is up to, but he's been an angel at home and there haven't been any weird texts, phone calls or anything else. There was one awkward moment, at the team Christmas party. One of the wives, Melanie Vashnov, asked me how I was coping. I looked at her like she was nuts and she said she knew about Cody fooling around—all the wives did—but she didn't like to gossip. She just wanted me to know she was available if I needed to talk because she understands being talked about.

Melanie has a crossed eye. She's really pretty, with a killer figure, but that crossed eye gives her an odd look sometimes and because she's shy in general, she appears standoffish and rude. It doesn't help that her husband is a big, burly Russian guy, Vasily, who doesn't speak English for shit and yells. All the time. They're a really odd couple, but he seems to adore her and she seems to need someone like him to protect her. One of the girlfriends said something mean about her and the other wives started to giggle. It made Melanie cry and when Vasily found out, he literally blew a gasket. He called out the husbands of every one of those women and shamed them right there in the middle of a party. The guy who was dating the woman that said it actually broke up with her—it was hard core.

I was still shocked that she said something to me. I thanked her and told her we were okay, but that I really didn't want to talk about it. Then I told Cody. I don't get involved in anything that could affect his job—other than CJ, that's always our top priority. He said not to worry, he would handle it. I don't know what that means, but I trust him. He's done some things I haven't liked, but he's never lied to me and he knows that I would never do anything that would haunt him at work.

All that said, I'm just keeping my head down, taking two online classes this semester and trying to be the best mom and platonic partner to my husband I possibly can be. I can't feel sorry for myself anymore. It's been too long, and frankly, as sad as I've been about everything, it takes way too much energy to be sad and angry all the time. I want to be happy again. And honestly, I'm going to try to make my husband notice me. I don't know how, exactly, but there has to be a way to start over from the romance perspective. We started with friendship—really good, true, genuine friendship. Then we had drunk sex followed by pregnancy and marriage.

We faked the romance in our marriage initially, but I drove a wedge between us because I let Brian's memory be the elephant in the room. It seemed like he was willing to try, so there might be a chance he wants to again. It might take a while to get there, but I'm going to focus on being his best friend. With Sergei back in Russia and Dom always in trouble lately, I think he's lonely. He has friends on the team, but those guys aren't like the friends he had before, which leaves me. I can do it, right? I can be his wife, partner, best friend and the mother of his child. Because I'm awesome. And somehow, some way, I have to make him think so again too.

19

## MAY, 2010

The team didn't make it to the playoffs so we're going on vacation early this year. I think it's more about getting Dom out of town than anything we need, but whatever it takes to help Dom is okay with me. He's been such a mess lately. He literally beat the shit out of a guy a few weeks ago—on the ice. What a nightmare. In trouble with the team, in trouble with the league, and possibly in trouble with the cops. They haven't decided if they're pressing charges or not. Since Cody's season was already done, he flew out to see what he could do but Dom was pretty belligerent and unresponsive. Instead, Cody called me and said to plan a family vacation—with Dom. I've got us booked at an all-inclusive resort in Jamaica and Cody said Dom is going whether he wants to or not. I'm not sure how that's going to go over since Dom can be a jerk when he wants to, but that's between them. I just did the planning.

It makes me sad to see what's happened to our tight little group since college... Brian's gone, of course. Sergei and Maria moved to Russia and now are divorced (they never should've gotten married, but that's beside the point), Cody and I are living in a weird, platonic, co-parenting marriage that's neither good nor bad (the marriage, not us personally, although that may apply to some degree as well). And Dom is this huge, gorgeous, fucked-up package of raging anger and guilt. He doesn't date (I'm sure he has sex, but those puck bunnies don't do him any good), doesn't have any friends outside of us and every time I talk to him he's more and more distant. I really hope us getting away together can help. I don't know what to do for him. Despite our problems, at least Cody and I have each other. And of course having CJ means we don't get to wallow in pity—we have to get up and parent. Like it or not. It seems like Dom has nothing to live for...

There's also the little problem of me never telling Brian's parents about CJ. I keep meaning to, wanting to, but it never feels like the right time and having a secret this big means we've pulled away from them. I miss my chats with Andra, and I know Cody would love to be able to talk to Brad about hockey and how his career is going. Brad's not in Boston anymore, he's moved up to an AHL team. We exchange Christmas cards now, but nothing else. I have to figure out how/when to tell them. CJ is getting bigger and they've already missed so much... sometimes the guilt is excruciating.

One issue at time, though. First we have to see what we can do for Dom. I hope it doesn't screw up our vacation, but it would be worse for Cody than for me because if I need an escape, I always have CJ as an excuse. Cody's stuck with him because, obviously, we invited him and made him go and that could be problematic. Not today, though. Today I'm going shopping for a new bikini. My husband might not be sleeping with me, but I'm sure going to do everything in my power to make him want to.

## 20

JUNE, 2010

I'M SITTING ON THE BALCONY OF OUR SUITE AT THE RESORT IN Jamaica, having a cup of coffee and writing this while everyone else is still asleep. We've been here three days and I think, maybe—fingers crossed!—Dom is starting to settle down. He and Cody had a knock-down, drag-out, nearly-came-to-blows fight the night before we left. I had to intervene and tell them they were scaring CJ. That was a lie—I had him in our room with the TV on as loud as I dared—but it worked and they both backed down. Dom stalked into the guest room, slammed the door and didn't come out all night, but in the morning he was showered and packed, ready for Jamaica.

He sulked on the plane and the first day we were here, but I swear, children are a blessing in so many ways. CJ walked up to him the next morning after breakfast and said, "Uncle Dom, are you too mad to play with me today?" And Dom's face kind of crumpled, like that really broke his heart. He said, "Of course not—I always want to play with you. What are we doing?" CJ said, "Mommy and Daddy say I'm too little to surf—will you teach me? Please? You can tell Mommy after we're done... pretty please?" Dom tried not to laugh, because we were just a few feet away so he knew we could hear, and he said, "Sure, bud. But we have to be really careful because your mom will drown me if you get hurt."

Meanwhile I was giving him the nod, letting him know it was okay, and making CJ think his dad and I were oblivious. It was the best thing that could have happened. Those two surfed for six hours. Like straight through lunch, no nap… and Dom was on top of everything. He made sure CJ reapplied sunscreen, he had his life jacket secured the whole time, and they bonded like nothing I've ever seen. It was so beautiful. Cody and I watched from a cabana where CJ couldn't see us and it was just wonderful. Afterwards, when CJ was so tired he could barely move, I gave him a bath and put him down for a late nap while Cody and Dom sat on the patio and talked.

Dom's been much more relaxed since then, and yesterday he and Cody went deep sea fishing. I opted out—I can't think of much I'd rather do less than be on a hot boat in the middle of the ocean with a bunch of guys drinking beer—and played with CJ at the kids' pool and play area. We had a nice dinner on the beach, talking and laughing like old times and Dom watched CJ for a little while so Cody and I could dance. It really feels like we're getting close again, but I'm not going to rush anything. We both need to be on board for trying again and I don't think he's there yet.

Later today, Dom is taking CJ again so Cody and I can get a couples' massage and have a quiet lunch alone. I feel kind of bad that Dom is acting as a stand-in babysitter, but it seems to be good for him and he volunteered, so it's not like we coerced him. He hasn't said a lot about anything important, but he did mention that he feels calmer when he's with us. I think that has a lot to do with CJ, so I'm going to encourage them to spend as much time as possible together. And maybe that will give Cody and I more time together too.

## 21

## DECEMBER, 2010

Sometimes it feels like every time I take a step forward, I not only go backwards, I go five or six steps back. Things have been so good, but yesterday proved just how precarious my marriage really is. It turns out that Cody is fooling around again. Not like before—he's been careful and discreet and I never would have known if he hadn't caught me masturbating. Yup. CJ was at school, he was at practice and I was having a little alone time. I had the TV on so I didn't hear him come in and he walked right into our room. He froze, I yanked up the sheet and neither of us spoke for a few seconds.

Then he sighed. Like this really long, deep, disappointed sigh that had him second-guessing his whole life. He looked so sad, it made me feel ashamed, but dammit, I haven't had sex in a long time! He started to walk away but I called out to him and he stopped, even though he didn't turn around. I told him I was sorry, that we weren't together that way and I still had needs. You know what he said? He said, "I can't believe you prefer a battery-operated piece of plastic over me." I was so shocked I couldn't even respond, but then he left the room and a minute later I heard the garage door opening. He didn't come back until late, but I was up and I knew right away he'd been with some-

one. His clothes were a little rumpled and he smelled faintly of
perfume… I just broke down, couldn't stop crying. I was so
upset, which made him upset, and then—I couldn't believe it—
he got emotional too. He didn't cry, but his eyes got a little
watery when he told me that he'd always love me, he just
couldn't live like a monk. The idea that I would rather mastur-
bate than be with him told him that there was no chance of us
having a sexual relationship again, so he would take care of his
needs in the most private manner possible.

I wanted to scream that I loved him, that I wanted him to
touch me, but this wasn't the time. If I'd done it then, it would
have seemed jealousy-induced and that wasn't good for us long-
term. So I came up with a compromise, asked him if we could
work up to it, if we could start from scratch. He seemed really
reluctant at first, but I wrapped my arms around him and told
him I wanted us to try. He hugged me back and said yes, even
though I don't think his heart was in it. I think he's given up on
me, but in the heat of the moment I didn't want him to think I
was having a knee-jerk reaction to what he'd done.

We've agreed to one date night a month, depending on
hockey of course, with no sex. We were going to literally go
back to the beginning, get to know each other outside of our life
as co-parents. We were actually going to have conversations like
we would have if we didn't already know so much about each
other. Obviously, we're not going to pretend we don't know each
other's families and such, but we're going to try to talk about
things like what high school was like, the day he'd been drafted
by the NHL, our first sexual experiences, etc. On date night, the
rules would be (barring an emergency) no talk about Brian, our
time in college, or CJ. All topics would be 100% new.

There would also be no sex for at least six months, or until
we'd made some kind of break-through in our relationship. I
don't know what that means—that part was his idea, not mine—
but I'm willing to do anything to make this work. Part of me
wants to just tell him, but I'm afraid if I do he'll be in a situation

where he kind of has to say he feels the same way, even if he doesn't. I don't want that. As much as I want him to love me back, it has to be organic. Otherwise, we're no better off than we are now. The only way I can do this is if he loves me; really, truly loves me.

## 22

APRIL, 2011

ANOTHER SEASON ENDED EARLY FOR CODY AND THE TEAM. HE'S really frustrated and there's nothing I can say or do to help because, obviously, it has nothing to do with me. Normally I can talk him off the ledge with anything related to hockey, but this time I don't know what to say. He's bored and I think he's going to put out feelers to see if anyone else is interested. I told him I'd like to go back to the U.S. and he said that was his preference too, assuming he could get a good contract. I think he'd like to play for Minnesota, since that's home, but I don't know that I could handle being that close to his family. They're nice, and we get along, but I can't help but wonder if they resent me or think I ruined his life.

On the personal front, our date nights haven't really happened, but it's truly been a comedy of errors. In December, he was on the road so much we couldn't find a time to do it, and then between Christmas, family in town for the holidays and CJ's birthday, we just never made it happen. January was a cluster-fuck of epic proportions... We planned two separate nights out and both of them blew up. The first was because our sitter was a no-show, and apparently her parents not only grounded her, they took her phone and didn't believe her when she said she had to babysit. The second night, CJ came down with the flu and then I got it and—sure enough—Cody did too. Between the three of us, we were down for the count for three weeks.

February was brutal with the team's travel and practice schedule, a winter storm that had us house-bound for several days and a burst pipe that forced us out of the house and into a hotel for ten days! March was no better and now it's April. With hockey season over, you'd think we've have plenty of time to be together, but nope—he's been moping and kind of distant, CJ has a million things going on at school and my last semester of classes for my master's is out of control. It's been nearly three years and I was anxious to finish, so I decided I'd finish up now and be done before summer. It's crazy, though!

We did talk about things last night, and we're going to have two date nights a month during the off-season to make up for how many dates we had to skip. I'm kind of excited, but I really can't think about much of anything until I finish the semester. Three weeks and counting... I'm buried in my final thesis and exams and a million details, and I'm so grateful Cody has stepped up to the plate with CJ. In spite of everything, we really are a well-oiled machine on a day-to-day basis. Even though hockey takes up so much of his time, he's still a hands-on dad, and the moment the season is over, he doesn't hesitate to jump in. How can I not love this guy?

I'm kind of looking forward to summer this year. Dates with my husband—even if we're not having sex—make me feel a little giddy. I always enjoy when we do things as a family, and of course, we're going on vacation. We're going to Disney World in July. CJ's never been, and my mother is going to join us, so I can't even imagine how excited he's going to be when we tell him. I've only been once, so it's going to be fun for me too, but get this—Cody's never been either! As a kid, all of his vacations were hockey-related and he never had any reason to go once he started playing in the NHL. It's going to be like having two kids on the trip, which is part of the reason I asked my mother to go.

Well, if I don't finish this paper, I won't be going anywhere this summer, so I'm signing off for now. Hopefully the next time I make an entry, I'll have something exciting to talk about! Maybe I'll even have gotten laid by then…

2 3

# SEPTEMBER, 2011

DID I SAY I MIGHT HAVE HAD SEX BY THE TIME I CAME BACK TO my diary? Yeah, that hasn't happened and I can't deny how disappointed I am. It seems like Cody's holding back, no matter how good things have been between us. I actually asked him if he'd been sleeping around again, and he was affronted, really offended that I even had to ask him that since he'd given me his word that he wouldn't. So we're kind of back to square one, with us going on platonic dates and talking about anything and everything without having sex. He did kiss me the other night, though. It was hot and sexy, but then he pulled back, said the time wasn't right. Grrr. I almost jumped him right there in the garage.

On another note entirely, we might be leaving Toronto! Cody talked to Brad the other night and apparently Brad is in the running to be named Head Coach of one of the new NHL expansion teams. If they choose him, he asked Cody if he was interested in coming along. Cody said he had to talk to me, but the idea of going to Las Vegas is awesome! I'm totally down for that, and I think it would be good for Cody and I, too, a chance to really start over. He didn't say much, because nothing will happen until the team chooses the coach, but he seemed interested. I'm keeping my fingers crossed because I really believe this would be a great change for us. And being there with Brad and Andra would basically force me to tell them about their grandson. It's going to be hard, but I have to do it and if this happens, it would seem the fates are lining up in agreement.

It feels like we've been in limbo for a long time now, so the idea of moving—even if it's not to Vegas—has already taken root. Cody spoke to his agent about seeing if there's any interest, but there isn't much we can do just yet. Training camp starts next week and he's been ramping up his workouts to make sure he's in great shape. He wants to look good out there, both as a matter of pride and to give him an advantage if he had any interest from other teams. He told his agent Minnesota was high on his list, much to my chagrin, but it's not like I can say that out loud. It won't be bad, it would just be kind of weird. I think his parents would be around a lot, and I don't know how I'll feel about it.

It would be good for CJ, and probably good for Cody, but I don't know that having his family in our business would help our marriage. We're so close—so close to coming together, being together, being a couple… but we literally teeter on the edge every single day. For every good date we have, we lose ground again over something out of our control. Whether it's a sick kid, something going on with the team—it's always *something*. I just want us to be alone. I know it's terrible, but I desperately want to send CJ to my mom for like a month, so it's just Cody and I, with nothing but time to be together. That's not going to happen, obviously. He's in school, my mom works, the logistics would never work out, but I can still wish it. I jokingly mentioned it to Cody and his eyes actually got really dark and intense, as though he liked the idea too, but there's no way to make it happen yet. Maybe next summer.

It's kind of funny, now that I'm done with school I have all this time to think about stuff and I don't know what to do with myself. It was so nice having Cody home all summer—it's going to be hard when he starts playing again. Did I mention he bought me the most beautiful necklace as a graduation present? It's made of sky blue and white topaz, with diamonds, set in white gold. It's absolutely stunning. He said it reminds him of my eyes and I can't help fantasizing about wearing nothing but that necklace to bed with him. I don't know what I'm going to do if we can't figure out how to be a real couple. He's keeping an emotional distance, but he's not going anywhere—that's what confuses me. Why does he stay if he doesn't want me? Especially now that sex is off the table completely. We're not having it together and he's agreed not to get it elsewhere. That means the goal is for us to have sex, and he knows I need more from him than just the physical connection… what's he waiting for?

On that note, I'm going to bed. I'm not solving any of the world's problems tonight, so I might as well get some sleep.

2 4

# DECEMBER, 2011

I HAVEN'T WRITTEN AN ENTRY IN THREE MONTHS BECAUSE I'M just too discouraged to write anything. No sex, no advancement in our relationship and no signs it's coming. I was planning to talk to Cody about it, but he pulled a groin muscle just before Thanksgiving and now he's grumpy about that. Him being home with a minor injury is nothing like him being home for the summer. He's on edge, always watching video of the games, hanging out at the arena with the team... instead of resting and healing. This is his first real injury and he doesn't like it at all. I don't like it much either.

As far as everything else goes, no change. CJ turns six this month and he's cute as a button, doing well in school and always fun to be with. Thankfully, CJ manages to cheer Cody up so they're closer than ever. I'm the odd one out these days, but I can't say anything while Cody's freaked out about an injury.

So I shop. Cody's never said a word about what I spend or where I go, but even he noticed I'm spending more money than usual. It was kind of funny... he didn't comment directly, but asked me if my purse was new. I told him it was and he said it was nice. The next night, he asked if my shoes were new. I told him they were. He said they were nice too. I gave him a look, almost as if I was daring him to say anything else, and he didn't, but I know he was thinking it. Then, the funniest thing was this morning. I was getting ready to leave and he asked where I was going. I told him "shopping" and he said, "Again?" I looked him right in the eye and asked, "Is there something you'd like to do together?" His eyes got really blue and he stared at me for a long time. Then he chuckled and said, "lots of things, but not today. Have fun." He kissed me on the forehead and left the room. So I spent a shit ton of money on shit I might need if I ever had to start over on my own. It feels a little dishonest, but my patience has worn thin. If he doesn't want to make this work, I have to protect myself. He says he's not going anywhere, but how can he go this long without sex?

The good news is I also got the Christmas shopping done. Except Cody's gifts. I have nothing for him and I'm not really feeling like it either. It hurts the way he pushes me away. I was responsible for it before, but I've told him in every way I know how that I want to try to be a couple. And still nothing. I have no choice but to consider divorce if something doesn't change. Not until after the holidays, though. As for Christmas, I may stick some coal in his stocking. CJ would think it was funny, and Cody would laugh too, but it would probably sink in that I'm upset. Maybe he doesn't even care. All I know is how long it's been since he's touched me and that I'm lonely.

It was okay while we were communicating, but now he's gone silent. Even now that he's home, he feels really far away and I can't live this way. I love him, but not at the expense of my soul. We were doomed from the beginning, and I won't give up until I've exhausted every imaginable option, but I'm losing hope. Brian's been gone a long time and no one has loved me since he died. I thought I could survive without that kind of thing, and be happy with a good friend, but it's not enough. It's just not. Cody has a year. If he doesn't want to make a go of things by the end of 2012, we're done.

# 25

## MARCH 2012

HOLY SHIT, BRAD WAS NAMED HEAD COACH OF THE NEW expansion team in Vegas and Cody was the first person he called! He wants us to come to Las Vegas with him. It's hush-hush and unofficial, of course. There are all kinds of contract negotiations and the expansion draft and stuff, but he thinks it'll be fine. Toronto will need to protect their younger players so Cody can tell management he wouldn't mind being unprotected in the draft and it'll probably work out well.

Cody thought I'd be upset, but I'm not. I think a new start would be great for all of us. Being in a new city with mild winters is right up my alley, and it's kind of exciting to be part of an expansion team. Everything will be new, exciting, shiny… the team probably won't be very good for a while, but Cody doesn't mind. He's ready for a change too.

On the other hand, Dom got himself into a world of trouble last week. Nashville was playing Montreal and one of their rookies slashed him in the back of the knee. Dom went after him and smashed him into the boards. Hard. He broke his neck. The video is horrifying. And the worst thing is that Dom is gutted. Like practically unresponsive. Not answering his phone or texts, won't even talk to Cody. The league has suspended him indefinitely pending an investigation and a meeting with the Department of Player Safety. We don't know what to do. This could be the end of his career.

Cody talked to Brad about it and he said he'd talk to him. That's all we can hope for right now. I think Dom has finally hit rock bottom, and it's been a long time coming, but boy, he crashed hard. If the NHL doesn't let him play anymore, things are going to get worse because there's nothing else in his life. I hate the thought of him being in this situation, but maybe it's what he needs. And if Brad can somehow talk him into going to Vegas with us, that might be good for everyone.

Of course, Vegas opens up a whole other can of worms for me. Living in the same city as Brad and Andra means... it's time. I have to tell them about CJ. This is not only the perfect opportunity for me to see them, it's also the perfect opportunity for them to get to know and spend time with their grandson. Cody says it'll be fine, that they'll be so over-the-moon about having a grandson they'll forgive us for keeping him from them. I don't know about that, but it warmed my heart to hear him say "us." He includes himself in everything with me, like we're still in this forever, and it gives me hope. Hope that we'll work it out. Hope that he'll actually love me someday the way I've come to love him. Hope that I can stay. Because I really, truly don't want to be with anyone else.

Vegas is going to be our last chance. As much as I love him, with every passing day, I realize I can't stay married to a man that doesn't love me. I have to find love again, even if I have to move back in with my mom and work two jobs to take care of CJ. And even if I don't find anyone else, living with him like roommates when I'm crazy in love with him... *hurts*. There's no other way to describe it. I hurt when I watch him playing with CJ, on the ice, when we're out with friends. I want us to have the real thing and my gut tells me if we don't find it in Vegas, we won't find it anywhere.

# MAY 2012

IT'S BEEN TWO MONTHS SINCE I'VE HAD A CHANCE TO WRITE anything—but guess what??? We're in Las Vegas! It's nuts. Cody talked to Toronto's management as soon as the season was over in mid-April and told them he was willing to go unprotected in the expansion draft because he wanted to go to Vegas. They were amenable to the idea so we put our house on the market and rented one here in Vegas. We've been here three weeks and I already love it.

Our furniture just arrived on Friday we've been going crazy trying to unpack. CJ's already settled in school so Cody and I have spent every day together, working on the house, exploring Las Vegas and... hanging out. There's something brewing with us, I can feel it, but he's still holding back. We're sharing a bedroom and a bed, though, which is unexpectedly exciting. No sex yet, but we've been exhausted. We haven't stopped running around for a solid month. Everything happened so fast, and the scary part is, even though plans are in place, there's still a chance the unofficial deal will fall through. We're going on vacation as soon as we can but CJs still in school and—get this —Dom gets here the first week of June, which is next week. He and Brad worked out a deal with the NHL and Nashville.

He's on probation over the summer. He has to complete a certain number of hours in an anger management support group, see a therapist of their choosing (that's local to him, whether it's here or in Nashville) and check in with either his coach in Nashville or Brad, depending on what happens in the entry draft. But Nashville is ready to cut him loose and Brad wants him, so that seems to be a no-brainer. We all agreed—me, Cody, Brad and Andra—to do whatever we had to do to get him through the summer and through his probation. We were like family in college and we're going to do our best to help him, no matter what it takes.

He has to want it, though. He has to be willing to put the work into it. I don't know how he's doing since the incident, not really, although Cody's been talking to him every day. He said Dom's withdrawn, frustrated, quiet. And that's not like him. That's what worries me most... Dom is usually such a fun-loving guy. I've missed the guy he was in college and my biggest fear is we'll never get that Dom back. I guess all we can do is try.

Cody's going to rent a furnished apartment for him so Dom has a place as soon as he gets here. Cody said he sounds resigned on the phone, and I don't know if that's good or bad. I mean, if he's not truly sorry about what happened to that kid from Montreal... well, I refuse to believe it. Dom doesn't have a cruel bone in his body. I'd trust him with my life. Maybe he's still trying to get past what happened to Brian. Maybe he's pissed off at life in general. But he would never purposely hurt someone. I know this about him. Somehow, we have to get him past whatever has been going on. Vegas might be Dom's last chance too.

The only negative so far has been avoiding Andra. Cody told me she and Brad got here last week but we've honestly been too busy to see them and, frankly, every time I think about it, I get a little sick. I'm not ready to tell them they've missed six years of their grandson's life or that I hid something so huge from them.

They're going to be furious and they have every right to be. I fucked up in a big way with this, so there's no one else to blame and no excuses to be made—I have to suck it up. I'm just not ready. I might never be ready, but Cody said we'll talk about it soon. Once we get Dom settled. And the house. And go on vacation… shit, I'm tired.

2 7

JULY 2012

I HAVE THE BEST NEWS—I HAVE A NEW FRIEND. IT'S A CRAZY story how I met Molly, but it's been so long since I've had any kind of bestie. It started last month when Dom and Cody literally found her in a parking garage where her husband was hitting her. They rescued her and—get this—Dom took her back to his place so she could hide from her husband. Yup, he took a stranger to his apartment and she hid in his guest room for a couple of days before she had a miscarriage. And suddenly they were friends.

Then he brought her to me, to help with female stuff while she recovered, and we bonded. She's older than I am by about eleven years, but she's awesome. Smart and sweet and a great cook. She loves CJ, Cody thinks she's great, and I think Dom is falling for her. She's turning forty this month and he won't be twenty-nine until October—I can't wrap my head around it—but no matter what happens with them, it's so fun to have another woman to hang out with.

She's slowly getting on her feet, healing from both physical and emotional abuse, and I'm not the only one that loves her. Our friend Toli (Sergei's older brother) asked her out, which is crazy, and Dom got jealous, but Molly says they're all just friends. She likes Dom too, but it's probably a little soon for her.

He helped her file for divorce but her husband is a real prick. We've kept her pretty sequestered so he doesn't find her, but he's already tried to make trouble.

Dom and Toli are in Protector mode, determined to keep Molly away from her ex, but it scares me a little. Hopefully, they can get some kind of restraining order if he keeps trying to find her. In the meantime, it's been fun to have someone to go shopping with and lay out with and drink wine with. I hadn't realized how much I'd missed female companionship until now.

## OCTOBER 2012

OH. MY. GOD. I DON'T EVEN KNOW WHERE TO START. I DON'T have a lot of time to keep up with this diary but this is important enough for me to write a long one.

First and foremost—CODY AND I ARE TOGETHER! Like full-on, in love, having sex, can't stop touching each other, every minute of every day. We got drunk a few weeks ago and wound up getting naked and the next day I finally asked him if he would ever return my feelings. He said he already does and the rest, as they say, is history. And bonus? My period is late!

Second, Molly is finally divorced. Tim kidnapped her and Sergei, who's finally back in the US, and the guys rode in there like fucking superheroes. It was pretty awesome. Scary while it was happening, but really great that they went and got them like that. Tim is in jail, the divorce is FINAL, and—more great news —Molly is pregnant too. We're due a week apart! She's scared, of course, after so many miscarriages, but so far so good. June babies for the win!

And Cody…oh my god, Cody. I love this man so much. I sat down outside a few weeks ago, when Cody was at practice, and I had a conversation with Brian. Yes, I know he's dead. Yes, I know his remains are in Boston. But he was Catholic and believed he would go to heaven, so I like to think he's up there looking down on me even though I'm not much of a believer… but I told him what was going on. That I'd always love him and that Cody and I would take the very best care of his son. That he was my first true love, and I'd never forget him. That I never would have looked at another man if he'd lived.

Then I told him goodbye. I cried a little, explaining that he'd been gone now longer than we'd been together, and that while I'd never forget what we shared, it was time for me to move on. With Cody. And I swear, non-believing heathen that I am—I felt a cool breeze ruffle my hair. Brian used to ruffle my hair because he knew it annoyed me at first, and then it just made me laugh. So he ruffled my hair one last time. I think he was telling me it's okay, that he approves. I really hope so, because I love Cody so much. Did I already say that?

It's important enough to repeat. Every once in a while there's a glimmer of guilt, where I think about him and how close we all were and how he would feel if he saw me with Cody—and then I remember that it never would have happened. Not in a million years, if he'd lived. And that makes it okay. Cody and I talked about it too, about how long we'd waited to allow ourselves to feel the way we do. To be a couple. To fall in love. We're going to renew our vows at some point, but for now, we're taking things one day at a time.

## APRIL 1, 2013

EIGHT YEARS, BRIAN. I CAN'T BELIEVE YOU'VE BEEN GONE eight years. You would have been thirty today. And I'm seven months pregnant. The last six months have been some of the best of my entire life, and I hope you're happy for me, wherever you are. Somehow, I know you are, because my heart is so full.

You'll be glad to know we told your parents about CJ—finally—and they adore him. They're truly the best grandparents in the world and I know that must make you happy. CJ is a happy, healthy, spoiled little boy with two full sets of grandparents and an extra grandma to boot (my mom). He's smart and loves hockey just like you do—Brad and Cody and Uncle Dom spend a lot of time skating and shooting with him. You'd love it.

For your birthday tonight, we're having cake for dessert because CJ asked when your birthday was and said we should celebrate. I thought maybe Cody would be upset but he wasn't, so I baked your favorite red velvet cake and we're going to sing to you tonight. I hope that's allowed in heaven.

I have more besties now too. The guys on the Sidewinders are falling in love right and left and it's been awesome. Drake Riser met a US Marine named Erin and they not only eloped, but are expecting a baby in October. Karl Martensson, who's our back-up goalie, is dating one of Erin's friends, a woman named Kate, and that's looking serious too. So one Sidewinder elopement, three Sidewinder babies coming up, and maybe a couple of weddings later this year too. And it's only April.

That's all I have time for today, but happy birthday, dear Brian. I miss you.

# OCTOBER 2013

I'D FORGOTTEN HOW MUCH WORK A NEWBORN IS! AND NOW she's almost four months old. But Avery has been such a delight in our lives. CJ thinks she's the cutest baby ever (and she's pretty darn cute with her white-blond hair and bright blue eyes) and Cody, well…he's truly over the moon. It's good she came in the summer, though, because she doesn't sleep for shit. I'm up at least three or four times a night because she's colicky, but it's getting better. I can't breastfeed—my milk makes her gassy—so now we're trying soy. I didn't want to, but we have to sleep. Especially with hockey season starting back up.

I have a great support system here in Vegas, though. Between Molly (even though she's a new mom too—and don't get me started—they named him Brian!) and Erin (who's pregnant) and Kate (Karl's new wife), there are a lot of friends to help out when I need it, no matter what's going on. It's different here than it was in Toronto. It's hard to explain, because everyone was nice there, but this group is…special. The guys have become an incredibly tight-knit unit and the WAGs so far have been epic. There's a few I don't know very well, but most of them are lovely.

On a sad note, one of our coaches, Dave Marcus, died of a

heart attack early in the summer so we've also been rallying around his widow, Tiff. She's tall and gorgeous and getting her Ph.D. in psychology, but the loss has been hard on her. She has twin toddler boys at home, who keep her busy, but I feel really bad. I'm just so busy with Avery it's hard to do anything for anyone else. We try to invite her out or go to her place when the guys are home, so we can be there for her too. It's been a struggle in that department. I can't imagine losing Cody. I think they'd only been married three or four years, and he was twenty-five years older than her, but still.

I think Zakk Cloutier, one of young D-men, has a crush on her, but I also think Jamie Teller does too. He and his movie star fiancée Rachel ended their engagement so he's been sniffing around Tiff. They're all being respectful because it's only been four months, but I hope she doesn't grieve too long. I know first-hand how emotionally harmful that can be and don't wish it on anyone.

P.S. Toli met someone! Kate and Erin's friend from college, Tessa Barber, is in the middle of a divorce and she and Toli hooked up at a bar one night, not knowing they had mutual friends! How crazy is that? I'm willing to bet another player is going down to the marital route!

## FEBRUARY 2014

I FEEL LIKE I NEVER SIT DOWN TO WRITE ANYMORE, BUT LIFE IS A busy freeway with tractor trailers buzzing by from every direction. Between Cody's travel, games, and practices, CJ's hockey and school schedule, and Avery being an infant, I barely breathe most days. It's getting better, but I'm tired. Cody says we should get help but I feel weird about it. Yes, we have a cleaning service that comes twice a week, and I send Cody's stuff out to the dry cleaners so I don't have to deal with it, but I can't imagine hiring someone to drive CJ to school or take care of Avery.

I'm considering a mommy's helper for one or two afternoons a week when the team is traveling because I don't want to spend the time when Cody is home doing things like grocery shopping. And it's so hard with Avery. She's into everything and we're still dealing with a little colic. It's better, and she's sleeping better, but she's still up once around two or three in the morning, and then I have to be up with CJ at seven, so having a break once in a while would be great.

Dom and Molly are already talking about having another baby since Molly's forty-one now and her biological clock is definitely ticking. I don't think I could do it this soon, but she doesn't really have a choice. I'm excited for her, though. After all the miscarriages she suffered because of her husband's abuse, she deserves this. And Dom and she are so good for each other. I've never seen him so happy. He loves being a dad and a husband, and he's never been better on the ice. It makes me so happy.

And Toli and Tessa are back together—did I even write about them breaking up? There's an August wedding planned, so here we go again…

32

———

# JUNE 2014

THE SIDEWINDERS WIN!
THE SIDEWINDERS WIN!
THE SIDEWINDERS WIN!

HOLY FUCKING SHIT, THE SIDEWINDERS WON THE STANLEY CUP! What a roller coaster ride this season has been, but it was abso-fucking-lutely amazing. Watching them lift that Cup and skate around the ice brought tears to my eyes. I couldn't help but think of Brian, wondering if he was watching, celebrating with his buds. He, Sergei, Cody, and Dom were inseparable in college, and this was their fantasy. They talked about it ALL THE TIME. Even though they knew it wasn't realistic to think they'd ever do it together since they'd all been signed to different teams, they fantasized about it.

I'm so proud of them and we partied way too hard last night, but... as always, it seems, there's some drama in the ranks. Marco Rousch, our douche of a starting goalie, kidnapped Tiff! It's fucking nuts—he just took her! We believe he blackmailed her into going with him to Switzerland, but we don't know anything else. She and Zakk have been dating for a couple of months, and he doesn't know what to do.

None of us know what to do.

A group of them gathered at Dante's house since the finals were in Philadelphia, but I don't know much beyond that. Zakk's sister, Danielle, is going to help him with the twins until they figure it out, but it's really scary. After Karl's ex, Therese, tried to kill him last year, we're getting a little freaked out about all this stuff happening to people on the Sidewinders. Brad said next season, he's locking them all in their houses at night… I wish that could work. I really hope we find out something soon. I'm worried about her.

**J**uly 2014:

**J**ust a quick update: Zakk found Tiff and brought her home! And—take a wild guess who's pregnant? Looks like there's going to be another Sidewinder baby in January! Almost makes me want one more. *Almost*.

## 33

## AUGUST 2014

MY FINGERS ARE GETTING A WORKOUT BUT HOW COULD I NOT make an entry about Toli and Tessa's wedding. As if attempted murders and kidnapping weren't bad enough, the wedding was an absolute nightmare. Marco showed up with a group of thugs, murdered Toli and Tessa's wedding planner, and shot Toli! Toli's okay, just a shot in the shoulder, but we were all terrified. Then, that fuckhead tried to kidnap Tiff again. Erin got a gun from one of the security guards who'd been shot and she killed Marco... but not before he shot her first.

Erin's in rough shape. Still in the hospital, very weak, we don't know what's going to happen. I've never been so terrified in my life. We were all just sitting down to dinner and then shit hit the fan. Cody's my hero, though. He literally shoved me under the table, pushed me onto my stomach and then got on top of me—so if bullets started flying he would protect me. I've never been more in love with him than I am right now. I tried to make him stop, but he wouldn't, and the whole time he was just covering me and holding me and whispering in my ear that he wasn't going to let anything happen to me.

Have I mentioned how much I love this man?

I think once we know Erin is okay and doesn't need

anything, we're going to go away for a few days, just the two of us. My mom said she would come watch the kids. But this summer has been really stressful, so we could use a few days alone to get our heads on straight again. I love him and our friends and our life here, but between the shootings and kidnappings, I'm a little freaked out.

The truth is—we all are. Toli thinks what happened at the wedding has something to do with his father back in Russia, but he's not saying much and Tessa told us it's better if we don't talk about it. The only good thing is that Fuckhead is dead so we don't have to worry about him anymore.

# APRIL 2015

As usual, it's been a while, and there's so much to catch up on… let's see, where do I start?

Toli's ex—Sergei's wife Tatiana—died under mysterious circumstances while Toli and Tessa were on their belated honeymoon in Russia. I didn't even ask for details because it's scary. And I'm kind of done with drama. But…

Vladimir Kolnikov, whom none of us know very well because his English isn't great, is dating Rachel Kennedy— Jamie Teller's ex. It seems serious.

And then… Brock Lassiter met one of Rachel's actress friends and they eloped. Like after a couple of weeks. I don't even know what's happening with all of this, but Ashleigh is nice. She and Rachel aren't like what I'd expect movie stars to be like, so they're a nice addition to the WAGs club.

Tessa got pregnant on her honeymoon and is due any day now.

Kate is pregnant with twins.

Dante's wife, Becca, just found out she's pregnant.

Tiff and Zakk aren't married yet, but they had a baby girl named Savannah in January. And get this—Zakk is legally changing his name from Zakk Cloutier to Zakk Marcus-Cloutier, to honor the twins' late father, Dave. We all sobbed when he told us.

Jamie is involved with—*Viggo*. I had no idea he was bisexual, but there you have it. And they are adorable together.

Erin is pregnant again.

Oh, and yes, before I forget. I'm going to have another baby this fall.

Cody is pretty fucking excited, if I do say so myself. I think even more than when we were pregnant with Avery. I'm excited too, though I'm not looking forward to all the weight gain and swollen ankles and all that. CJ, on the other hand, thinks it's gross and says one baby is more than enough. He makes me laugh. He complains about Avery, but he's the first one to go to her if she starts to cry, so I suspect he's going to be a great big brother no matter how many more we have. I think three kids is plenty, but you never know!

I hope Cody's not disappointed if it's another girl, but deep down in my heart of hearts, I want girls. CJ is our son, Brian's son, and I never, ever want him to play second fiddle to another son. Cody has never behaved like CJ wasn't his. Not before he knew and not now, but I worry a little. And I worry about Brad too. He and Andra are CJ and Avery's grandparents, but I wonder how they'll feel about a son.

Maybe I'm just hormonal and overthinking things. I just want us all to be happy. God knows, there's been enough drama the last few years for a soap opera. Huh. Maybe Rachel and Ashleigh could star in it.

Kidding.

Sorta.

## 35

## DECEMBER 2015

I cannot believe my baby boy is eight today! EIGHT! I still remember the panic and horror and shame I felt the day I took that first pregnancy test. I thought my life was over, that Cody would never want me or our baby. It never occurred to me Brian and I had an accident because, well, we'd been together over three years and never had one before. The worst part back then was not being able to ask him. Had there been a condom malfunction? I'd been allergic to birth control, so we always just used condoms but we were careful. I'd been clear I intended to finish college…but this was right before graduation. I would have finished college regardless, and Brian knew that.

Those early days were so full of hurt and grief and shame and so many other emotions, it's hard to remember what I was feeling or thinking. But the first time they put him in my arms, I knew I was in love. And I still am. He's older now, incredibly smart and independent, and he's a goalie, just like his dad. But he's a good kid, loves and protects his sisters fiercely, and loves hockey more than even Cody. He'll spend hours watching film, whether it's Sidewinders stuff or anything he can find online about Brian. I have no doubt we have another pro in the making…and all his Sidewinders uncles feed the beast.

He's close to Brad and Andra, to Cody's parents, and adores my mom (Grammy Pammy). There's a lot of love in this house, and there's one more to love now too. Ella was born in September and even CJ is a little excited about her. He wants to hold her all the time. I'm pretty sure Avery doesn't give a shit about the loud new baby, but she might come around. Ha ha

And I guess I should update all the new happenings around here, because it never ends…

Kyle and Kendall Martensson were born. Right after Kate was in a horrible car accident. Thank God everyone is okay. She was in a coma for five days and Karl was out of his mind with grief. He refused to see the babies until she woke up. It's a good thing she did. We were pretty scared and Erin didn't leave her side, even as pregnant as she was.

Tessa gave birth to Alexei and Toli is over the moon. Tessa mostly wants to sleep, and I can't say I blame her. We're all trying to help out because the babies around here are coming hard and fast!

Jamie and Viggo got married in Canada. They're so amazing together, I wish them a lifetime of joy. Did I tell the story of how Jamie got beat up by a group of white supremacists who almost killed him? No? Maybe next time. It's a long story.

Brock and Ashleigh are pregnant, expecting early next year, and they're adopting the little girl Ashleigh has been fostering, Bella. Her adult older sister, Angel, is also joining the family, though in an unofficial capacity.

Dante and Becca had a little boy they named Dylan. It was a pretty emotional time for Dante after his late fiancée and the son she carried, whose name was Louis, were killed. I don't know Dante that well, but he tends to be a moody, serious guy and I don't think he's stopped smiling since Dylan was born. He says he wants three more. Becca smacked him. Time will tell, but I have a feeling there will be lots more babies…

Also, one of the rookies on the team, Zaan Hagen, is living with us. The team likes 18-year-old rookies to live with a veteran player if at all possible, so we're like his much older big brother and sister. Luckily, he's a good kid who also loves OUR kids, so it hasn't been a problem at all. He's adorable so I have a feeling he won't be on the market long at all.

And finally, Vlad and Rachel are getting married on their mutual birthday—January first. Hopefully, it will be a much less "exciting" event than Toli and Tessa's wedding.

3 6

NOVEMBER 2016

YEAH, HAVING A TODDLER AND A NEWBORN MEAN NO TIME FOR Mom to write in her diary. I know, it's been eleven months, but I'll try to make this entry worthwhile. Let's see… what's happened in the Sidewinders world since I last checked in?

Jamie and Viggo added a baby to the family. Viggo's ex-wife, Emilie, had a baby for JAMIE, so that Viggo's daughter Simone and the new baby (a son named J.J.) would have the same mother. So they could always be a family. Even though she's now dating an ex-MI6 agent named Darryl Carruthers, who goes by the nickname Chains. I don't even want to know what that stands for. But I love their extended family. I think what they're doing is beautiful.

Zaan is in love with Coach Rousseau's 18-year-old daughter, Lexie. I don't know how that's going to end, but he's living in an apartment now, and Lexi's in New York in college, which means it might already be over. Lexi's a sweet girl who's been through a lot. She had breast cancer at sixteen, so Rob is a little overprotective. I think they're so young to be in love, but Brian and I were the same age when we fell in love, and I have no doubt we would still be together if he hadn't died.

Dmitri Papadakis has been dating Brock and Ashleigh's

pseudo-daughter (Angel) on the sly and we all just found out she's pregnant. Brock was pretty pissed, but Dmitri says he loves her. There's some drama with his old-fashioned Greek father, and I haven't heard the whole story.

Tiff is pregnant again too, which is kind of hilarious, but I think they wanted all the kids to be closer in age. They're engaged but not in any hurry to get married, which is cool with me. Tiff went through a lot with Marco and she's probably taking her time with big life changes.

As for me and Cody, well, life is so much better than I ever thought it would be. Last night, he got home late from a road trip but had stopped at Tiffany's in NYC and bought me jewelry. Not just some earrings or something, but a matching set of necklace, earrings, and bracelet. Gold with diamonds and sapphires, which he says match my eyes, and they're stunning. No reason, no birthday or anniversary, just because he loves me. And it's so unnecessary. But spectacularly sweet and romantic. Just like him.

## OCTOBER 2017

I THINK MY DIARY-WRITING DAYS ARE COMING TO AN END. I JUST don't have the time, and since CJ can read and write now, I keep it hidden. Not that I have any huge secrets, but I'd never want him to know just how much Cody and I struggled in the beginning of both our marriage and his life. Seeing how much I loved and missed Brian wouldn't be a bad thing, but I wouldn't want him to know how hard it was for Cody and I to find each other. And my life is a busy, happy merry-go-round of life and love and adventures and hardship. No relationship, no one's life, is perfect, but mine comes pretty damn close.

I have three of the best kids in the whole world. My husband is truly the greatest. My family, which includes mine and Cody's and Brian's, is amazing. And frankly, it would be idiotic of me to have anything to complain about. I still do once in a while, of course, but that's simply human nature. In reality, my life is a dream. I fall more in love with my husband every day. I know, that sounds ridiculous, but he's the whole package and I don't even try to pretend otherwise. I am a very lucky woman. Not just because I have the best life ever, but also because I was lucky enough to have found true love TWICE. Guilt over moving on is in the past now, and once in a while, when I go visit Brian at the cemetery in Boston, I tell him all the stories and make sure he knows how loved and happy CJ is. Not to mention, how he's never forgotten. Dom named his son Brian, CJ's middle name is Brian, and Brad and Andra honor him every day with the life they lead and the love they have for all of us.

CJ is becoming an amazing little goalie, and while Cody has made sure to expose him to all the positions, including a little coaching and reffing, CJ is a goalie through and through. But he's well-rounded and has subbed as a forward on other teams when a kid was sick or on vacation more times than I can count. It's ironic because he's fast—just like Brian was. And the older he gets, the more he looks like his father too. I hope, if there is such a thing as an afterlife, heaven, or whatever, Brian looks down on us with love and happiness.

I still miss him. But it's different now. It's a sweet, poignant set of memories from "before." Before Cody. Before our family. Before my life now. There's a picture of Brian and I, taken at the winter formal two months before he died. We are so gorgeous and happy and in love. I keep it in CJ's room so he always remembers that his mom and biological dad were in love and though he wasn't planned, he was wanted. I keep it so we all remember Brian, forever, but also know that it's possible to move forward after loss.

There are five pages left of this diary and I think maybe I'll add one or two more entries so that the book feels complete. I don't know when, but I'll be back at least once more. Thank you for listening to me all these years.

$$38$$

JUNE 2018

So I'm back less than a year later but it's a special entry and maybe the very best way to say goodbye to this journal I've kept for thirteen years.

I may not have mentioned it in earlier entries, but Toli's oldest son, Anton, was drafted by the Sidewinders. He went to college and last fall he started playing on the team. *WITH TOLI.* It was an amazing season that ended in the very best way— another Stanley Cup. Father and son. All of us up in the bleachers cried SO HARD when Cody handed the Cup to Toli and Toli then handed it to Anton. I think Toli and Anton cried too. Especially since Toli announced his retirement the next day. What an amazing career.

Twenty-two years in the league. Three Stanley Cups (he'd won one before he became a Sidewinder), two major hockey leagues (the NHL and the KHL), five beautiful children (four biological sons—Anton, Alex, Andy, and AJ, and Tessa's beautiful daughter Raina, who calls him Daddy and has no contact with her biological father). And who's probably going to be the best hockey player of them all, save Anton. Though she might give him a run for his money in ten years.

Brad retired too. His years coaching are over and he and

Andra plan to travel and spend as much time as possible with their grandchildren. They've embraced Avery and Ella like they were their own, so there's a lot of love in this house. I don't think Avery and Ella even understand how they have so many grandparents, but it doesn't matter. Love is love.

Since Brad knew he was retiring, he brought in an Associate Coach just for the playoffs. A former player named Jared Wylde. He's so freakin' hot it's ridiculous. And I don't say that lightly because I truly believe my husband is the hottest man on the planet. But Jared is a close second. And Brad brought him on because he wants him to take over for him. Jared's a hotshot college coach in Boston but they think they can get him to stay here, so we'll see what happens there.

Royce Lenahan has been dating Dmitri's sister Tina and their wedding is in a few weeks, so the guys are falling hard and fast, one at a time. Nate Calloway has been dating a sports writer named Chelsea Baldwin and they live together now so I figure that's another wedding coming sooner rather than later. And Tore Brekken, the team's current manwhore, has been dating one of Chelsea's friends. I can't believe he's ready to settle down, but love finds us when we're least expecting it.

Toli's brother Sergei also got married. To Zakk's sister Danielle. So she's living up in Alaska now and is the first female assistant trainer in the NHL. It's pretty cool seeing her behind the bench during games. And seeing Sergei so happy. He struggled so much after losing Tatiana, but even with ten years between them, he and Danielle bring out the best in each other. She's sweetness and light with some kickass hockey skills, and a master's degree in kinesiology, so she is no one to mess with. And Sergei and Tatiana's son, Niko, adores her. I'm so happy for them even though we hate that they live so far away.

So… there's one page left and I have a few final thoughts. I started this diary as a way to soothe my heartbroken, grieving, battered soul after I lost Brian. A safe place to talk about my hurt, my love, my yearnings, at a time when I felt lonelier than I ever had in my life. And now that need is gone. Maybe one day I'll buy another journal to write about my children, all the little details of their lives so I don't forget them, but I also have been scrapbooking, which catches most of that.

I don't know if there will be a sequel to this but my gut says no. I don't have anything to write about. All my major dreams have come true. Love. Family. Children. Friends. And while I could write about all those amazing good (and occasionally bad) times, it feels better to live it instead of writing about it.

This diary has been my companion for thirteen years and now I will lovingly wrap it up and put it away in a special box up in a corner of my closet. Someday, when I'm gone, I hope my children find it and read about my journey from Brian's girl to Cody's wife. From college brainiac to hockey wife and mom. From that underprivileged girl from bumfuck, South Carolina to a big city woman with an advanced degree I never used.

When and if you're reading this, my wonderful children, know that these last thirteen years changed my life. And brought you into it. I hope I've loved you well and taught you well and have always been there for you.

And my darling, Brian. I started this diary when I lost you. Writing it kept you closer to me and helped me work through every painful moment until the time came for me to move on. Thank you for loving me and for giving me CJ. He honors you, we honor you, and you are never forgotten. I hope those thugs that killed you have died awful, painful lives in prison. I hope there is an afterlife that includes hockey and beer. I love you always—Suzanne Cary Armstrong.

# ALSO BY KAT MIZERA

***Las Vegas Sidewinders:***

Dominic

Cody's Christmas Surprise

Drake

Karl

Anatoli

Zakk

Toli & Tessa

Brock

Vladimir

Royce

Nate

Sidewinders: Ever After

Jared

Dmitri's Christmas Angel

Ian

***Sidewinders: Generations:***

Zaan

Tore

Anton

***Alaska Blizzard:***

Defending Dani

Holding Hailey

Winning Whitney

Losing Laurel

Saving Sara

Chasing Charli

A Very Blizzard Christmas

Tending Tara

Calling Cassie

Playing Peyton

**_St. Louis Mavericks (with Brenda Rothert)_**

Hard Fall

Hard Limit

**_Lauderdale Knights:_**

Slap Shot

Big Shot

**_Rock Hard:_**

*Play*

*Pause*

*Rewind*

*Fast Forward*

**_The Royal Trilogy:_**

Nowhere Left to Fall

Nowhere Left to Run

Nowhere Left to Hide

**_Royal Protectors:_**

Sandor

Cocky Protector (book 1.5, part of the Cocky Heroes Club series)

Xander

Axel

Dax *(A Royal Protectors/Sidewinders crossover novel)*

### *Inferno:*

Salvation's Inferno

Temptation's Inferno

Redemption's Inferno

Tropical Inferno (formerly "Tropical Ice")

### *Romancing Europe:*

Adonis in Athens

Smitten in Santorini

Lucky in Lugano

### *Other Books:*

Special Forces: Operation Alpha: Protecting Bobbi (Susan Stoker's Special Forces World)

Special Forces: Operation Alpha: Protecting Delilah (Susan Stoker's Special Forces World)

View Kat's entire collection of books at www.KatMizera.com

# ABOUT THE AUTHOR

*USA Today* Bestselling author Kat Mizera was born in Miami Beach with a healthy dose of wanderlust. She's lived from coast to coast, and everywhere in between, but home is wherever her family is.

A devoted mom and wife to her wonderful and supportive husband (Kevin) and two amazing boys (Nick and Max), Kat loves to travel the globe with her adventurous, hockey loving family. Greece is at the top of that list. She hopes to one day retire there, spending her days writing books on the beach.

Kat is former freelance sports writer who now writes steamy hockey romance about her favorite fictional teams, the Las Vegas Sidewinders and the Alaska Blizzard. The library of novels she's penned also include sexy contemporary stories about baseball stars, alpha sex club owners, special forces heroes, rock stars and royalty. Regardless of genre, her books about bad boys with hearts of gold will steal your breath, rock your world and melt your heart.

WHERE TO FOLLOW KAT:

WEBSITE
FACEBOOK
TWITTER
INSTAGRAM

BOOKBUB
KAT'S PRIVATE FACEBOOK GROUP

www.ingramcontent.com/pod-product-compliance
Lightning Source LLC
Chambersburg PA
CBHW071437300726
48976CB00004B/1363